Polly PEACOCK

& The Pink Flamingos

For Ava, the littlest diva

Little Polly Peacock,
With a style that was her own,
Wasn't afraid to flaunt her feathers,
And let her colors show.

She wore a tutu and a boa,
Rain boots with big red spots,
A sparkly cape down to her toes,
And a bow with polka dots.

The boring pink flamingos,
With noses in the air,

Taunted Polly Peacock,
They pointed, laughed, and stared.

Polly cried alone for hours,
Before realizing she shouldn't care,

If she wanted to wear tutus and spots,
That was what she was going to wear!

One day Percy Pigeon,
Stopped by to chat and eat,
And mentioned to Polly Peacock,
That her outfit looked unique.

Polly danced and sang,
She flipped and bowed,
The other birds gathered,
And cheered so loud!

The boring pink flamingos,
Who all looked just the same,
Watched from across the water,
And envied her new found fame.

"Maybe she's not so weird,"
Said one flamingo to the rest,
"She seems to have a lot of fun,
Even though she's strangely dressed."

The flamingos grew more jealous,
They wanted attention too,
Now each flamingo wore a boa,
Rain boots, and a tutu.

Then the pink flamingos,
Tried to be the peacock's pal,
"But you were never kind to her,"
Said the wise and clever owl.

The flamingos lined up early,
For tickets to Polly's show,
They gulped and said "we're sorry",
As she saw them in front row.

All the birds got up on stage,
They danced, they twirled, they sang,
And could you guess who joined in?
The entire pink flamingo gang.

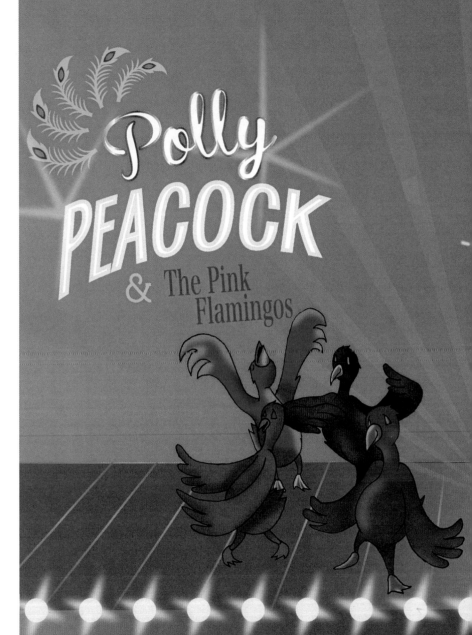

The boring pink flamingos,
Learned a valuable lesson that day,
Just because they prefer all pink,
Doesn't mean the other birds must
look that way.

The pink flamingos' noses came down,
And smiles began to grow,
Not only did they befriend Polly,
But also every pigeon and every crow.

Now every Sunday evening,
The birds gather at Percy Pigeon's nest,
All different beaks, claws, and feathers,
Coming together for a fancy fest!

The not-so-boring pink flamingos,
No longer live a life of pink,
And Polly continues to flaunt her feathers,
And embrace that she's unique.

THE

END

WHAT MAKES YOU STAND OUT FROM THE FLOCK?